FEAST FOR 10

CATHRYN FALWELL
CLARION BOOKS, NEW YORK

Clarion Books
a Houghton Mifflin Company imprint
215 Park Avenue South, New York, NY 10003
Text and illustrations copyright © 1993 by Cathryn Falwell
All rights reserved.

For information about permission to reproduce
selections from this book, write to Permissions,
Houghton Mifflin Company,
215 Park Avenue South, New York, NY 10003.
Printed in Malaysia

Library of Congress Cataloging-in-Publication Data

Falwell, Cathryn.
Feast for 10 / by Cathryn Falwell.
p.   cm.
Summary: Numbers from one to ten are used to tell how
members of a family shop and work together to prepare a meal.
ISBN 0-395-62037-6   PA ISBN 0-395-72081-8
[1. Counting.   2. Afro-Americans—Fiction.   3. Cookery—Fiction.
4. Family life—Fiction.]   I. Title.   II. Title: Feast for ten.
PZ7.F198Fe   1993
[E]—dc20
92-35512   CIP   AC

TWP   35 34 33 32 31 30
4500291464

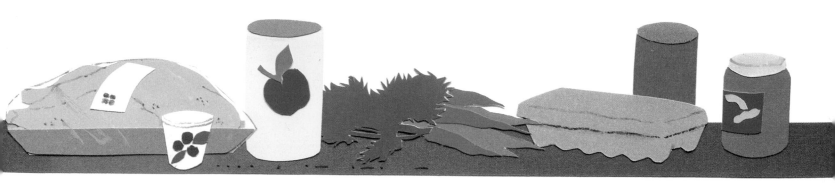

For
my family

in
loving memory
of
my grandmothers

Willie Mae McMullen Chauvin
and
Evelyn Haning Falwell

who often made
feasts for plenty

1 one
cart
into the
grocery
store

2 two
pumpkins
for pie

3 three
chickens
to fry

 four
children
off to
look for
more

5 five kinds of beans

6 six
bunches
of greens

 **7** seven
dill pickles
stuffed in
a jar

 **eight ripe tomatoes**

9 nine plump potatoes

10 ten hands help to load the car

Then . . .

1 one car home from the grocery store

2 two
will
look

3 three
will
cook

4 four
will
taste
and ask
for
more

5 five empty cans

6 six
pots and
pans

7
seven
more carrots
to wash
and
peel

8 eight
platters
down

9 nine
chairs
around

10 ten
hungry folks
to share
the
meal!